SHAKE A LEG

For Lesley Reece – J.O.
For Lance & Joy Riley – B.M.P.

First published in 2010

Copyright © text Boori Monty Pryor, 2010

Copyright © illustrations Jan Ormerod, 2010

Allen & Unwin
83 Alexander St
Crows Nest NSW 2065 Australia
Phone: (61 2) 8425 0100
Fax: (61 2) 9906 2218
Email: info@allenandunwin.com
Web: www.allenandunwin.com

Cataloguing-in-Publication data available from the
National Library of Australia
ISBN 978 1 74175 890 0

Designed by Jan Ormerod
Set in 14 pt MetaPlus Medium by Ruth Grüner
This book was printed in July 2010
at Tien Wah Press (PTE) Limited,
4 Pandan Crescent, Singapore 128475

3 5 7 9 10 8 6 4 2

Teachers' notes available from
www.allenandunwin.com

ALLEN&UNWIN

SHAKE A LEG

Boori Monty Pryor & Jan Ormerod

Three hungry boys are hunting for pizza in Far North Queensland.

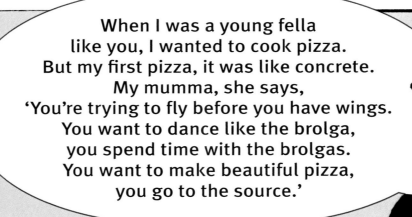

When I was a young fella like you, I wanted to cook pizza. But my first pizza, it was like concrete. My mumma, she says, 'You're trying to fly before you have wings. You want to dance like the brolga, you spend time with the brolgas. You want to make beautiful pizza, you go to the source.'

The tomato sauce?

Si! The source of the sauce – *Italia.*

For two years I lived with a family in a village. I had to make my sauce sin before I learned to make dough.

Buonissima!

Buona la salsa!

These boys went hunting for honey.

They could hear a hum from inside this tree so they cut the branch down.

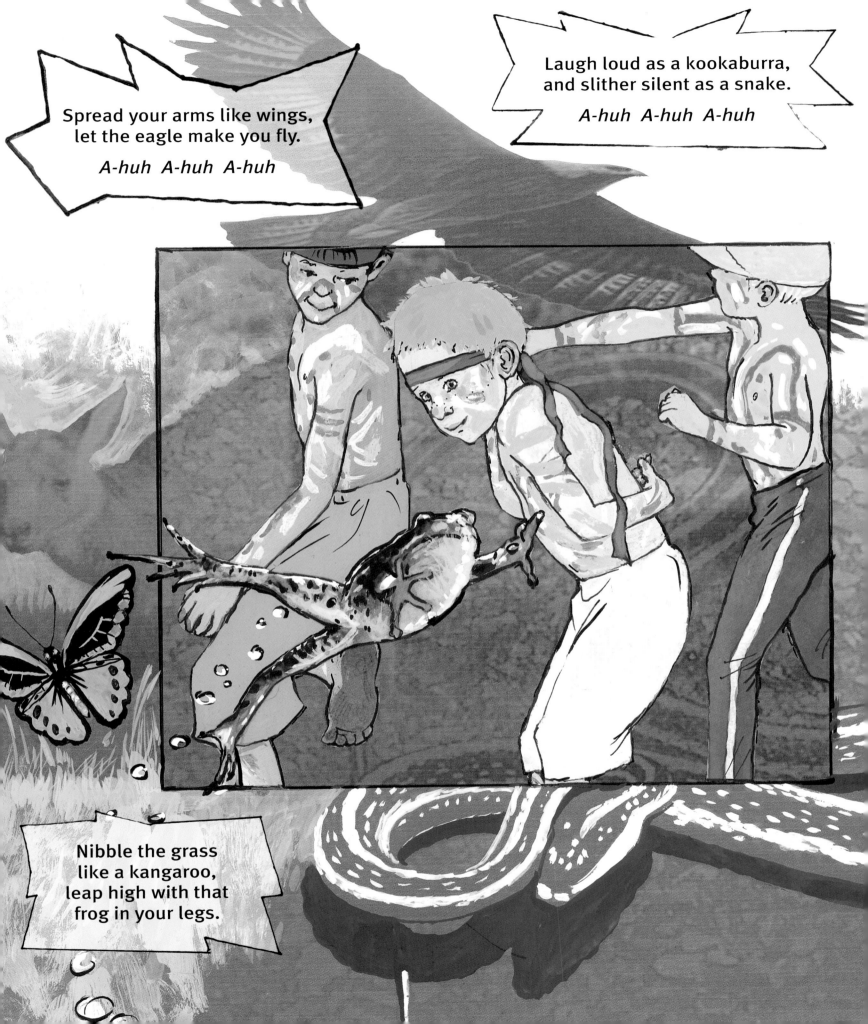

All you fellas watching,
come up, join in, *warrima*.

Clap your hands, little ones.

Stamp your feet, nannas.

Get down and dance,
you smart young things,
mummas and daddas.

A-huh A-huh A-huh

We've got the whole town
dancing!

This was once
our *bora* ground
our gathering place
for *warrima*.
Now it's a busy street
in this town.

Our pizza feeds the soul,
keeps you dancing strong,
lifting the dust with your feet,
listening with eyes, ears and heart
so our old people can join us
and together we *warrima*.

Stories swirling in the stars above,
dances rising from the earth below,
around the world our arms stretch wide
to *warrima*
to shake-a-leg
to welcome you.

Photograph © Ian Manning

ACKNOWLEDGEMENTS
Boori Pryor

The 'source' of this book is an amazing man, my cousin Lance Riley, who I learnt so much from. He was a proud Tjapukai man from the tablelands of North Queensland. He kept our culture strong through his family ways and his enormous struggle each day for his children to be part of their culture and for that culture to remain alive and growing. His children are in this book. Without them, the pages would be empty. I thank Bertie Riley, especially, for the inspiration he has given me to do my own dance, and the Brady Bunch, especially Graham and Jasmine, for their love and strength; and I am grateful for the western Gu Gu Yalanji land that holds the Laura Dance Festival – that bora ring continues to unite us all.

Jan Ormerod kick-started the book after we met at the Fremantle Children's Literature Centre and she was moved by the many photos I showed her of dancers at the Laura Festival. The beauty of Jan's work is beyond what I could ever have imagined, and I thank her for her great effort. I also thank Lesley Reece for creating space at the Centre for artists to have time to make dreams come true. And I thank Mailee Clarke for being a navigator through rough seas.

I thank Meme McDonald for her input into the making of this book. Meme has the amazing gift of being able to mix and move words in a story so that we can all sit down and read it together without fear. And in this book hopefully we can read and see the beauty and colour of an ancient culture in a new way.

I thank Erica Wagner, publisher, for her vision, her ability to see what can be and allow what will be to happen. She has been there all through the creation of this book and I deeply appreciate her commitment to our culture. This book was edited by Sarah Brenan, who was remarkable in her ability to remain patient and trusting throughout, gathering the many threads together. Ruth Grüner with her design expertise made the book sing in tune, and I thank her for this.

I thank Jenny Darling and Donica Bettanin for looking after this book, especially for believing in it in the early days; and Glen Leitch and all the hard-working team at Young Australia Workshop for keeping me travelling around Australia to schools each year. I thank each and every one of those schools, their teachers and students, for opening their hearts and for being willing to listen. This book belongs to you as well. Jan Deans, Phil Egan, Ian de Valder, Scott Anderson, Annabell Knight, Amanda Stewart and Louise Wilkinson are among those teachers and educators who have helped this book come to be and I thank you all for the dedication you have to helping future generations of people belong to the country they live in.

I thank Jose Montana and Andrea Rotondella for help in sourcing Italian images and language to enrich the text.

My family are in each page and share every step along the way of my life. To my parents, Dot and Monty Pryor, and my sisters Sue, Cilla, Chrissy, Chubby, Kimmy, Toni, Chicky and my brothers Kenny, Paul and Rosco – thank you. And to Mari and Ciaran Ward, Larry, Lou, Jalin and Summer Holmes, Andrea Jenkins, Julie and Jim Morrison, Tracey and Peter Petersen, Ashleigh and Philip, Peta and Ross Pettigrew, Chelsea and Joseph, Sussannah and Andrew D'Arcy, Declan and Imogen – thank you all for what you have given to this book as it grew.